Ulf Nilsson • Anna-Clara Tidholr

Goodbye, Mr. M

Translated by Nathan Large

Hawthorn Press

Here is an old guinea pig called Mr. Muffin. Mr. Muffin is
nearly seven and he is tired and grey. He lives in an upside-
down blue cardboard box that looks like a house, with a door
and a chimney.

Outside the house is a cardboard letter box. Sometimes there's a piece of cucumber or an almond in the letter box. Mr. Muffin always checks carefully to see if there's any post.

One Tuesday he finds a letter:

Mr. Muffin,
I am *so sad* because daddy *says*
that when guinea pigs get old
they might *suddenly die* ...

Can Mr. Muffin read? He eats up the letter.
The paper turns into flakes, like flurries
of snow.

Most of the time, Mr. Muffin sits in his blue house and sighs, and thinks about the life he's lived. When he was young, he dreamed of being soft, not plump; of being able to climb. He remembers a hamster who was soft as silk. He himself, he thought, was fat as a cow and bristly as a pig.

Once, Mr. Muffin was married to a lady guinea pig – Victoria, black as the night, beautiful as the day. Together they had six fluffy little children. Oh, they were the sweetest little things. Yes, those were the days! But they have all left home now and Mr. Muffin sighs.

They all went for a walk once. They wanted to see how far you could go in the world. They walked as far as the garden's furthest fence. All of a sudden they met a bird that narrowed its eyes and peered at them as if they were chipolatas. Mr. Muffin fainted with fright while the children watched over him.

That was the longest expedition ever, to the furthest reaches of the world. And it was Mr. Muffin and his six children who went there. They went to the end of the world, and saw there was an edge …

The hamster ran around in his wheel, round and round, but did he get anywhere?

But Victoria is long since dead. She was sniffing a flower when
a bee stung her on the nose.

Mr. Muffin tries to remember her funeral. She was buried in a shoe box at the bottom of the garden, wasn't she? Why are there bees?

Mr. Muffin has a stomach-ache now. He sits alone in his house and remembers, and makes a little list:

I've had a good life,
better than most:

One very clever and kind wife.

One little blue house with its own
letter box.

Six fluffy little children.

Three cuddles a day.
That makes 7665 cuddles in
my life.

728 whole cucumbers in my life.

2555 armfuls of grass, hay and dandelions.

And now and then some post
in the letter box.

One Wednesday morning Mr. Muffin can't get up. His stomach and legs hurt too much. A vet comes, and presses and pinches him so that he cries out.

And afterwards the vet shakes her head.

All day Mr. Muffin sits in his house, in a lot of pain. He looks at the walls, at the really good artwork hanging there.

A photo of Mrs. Victoria and all the sweet little children.

A picture of Mr. Muffin when he was young, strong and proud. He could carry a whole cucumber on his back!

He sits and thinks of an old song his father used to hum:

Time ticks by: with every beat
You eat as much as you can eat.

In the evening he goes out, slowly, to the letter box. No matter how sick you are, you should fetch the post.

There are three almonds in the letter box. And a letter with fifteen red hearts on it.

Daddy says that dying isn't bad,

you just go to sleep and the pain goes away.

It's over quickly and then you can rest.

Everyone dies – you, me, and daddy.

Maybe you get to meet your mother and

your wife?

But I'm not sure if there's a heaven ...

Mr. Muffin gnaws the letter to bits, like flakes, like flurries of snow. Suddenly he starts to sneeze. The flakes whirl about.

All night he lies there and sneezes and sneezes, and every time he sneezes his stomach hurts.

On Thursday morning he finds another letter, the last one:

Dearest Mr. Muffin!
I did not want to wake you
since you'd fallen asleep at last.
I hope you were not upset
by what I wrote yesterday.
I have been up all night, too,
lying in my bed and thinking about death.
I think that either you just get to rest,
and that's nothing to be scared of.
Or you go to heaven and
everything will be all right.
I hope you get to read all this.
Daddy says that you may have died
by the time I get back from school.
I love you so very much.

Mr. Muffin barely manages to nibble at a small corner of the letter. Then he feels a sharp pain in his stomach. It hurts dreadfully. He lies down.

And suddenly he is dead.

And all the newspapers will report the tragic news: the death of a guinea pig.

Our beloved
Mr. Muffin
has passed away suddenly

*The little guinea pig angel came,
smiled, then turned back again*

———————————————

The funeral will be held in a corner
of the garden

Mr. Muffin dead

Mr. Muffin passed away on Thursday morning. He was seven years old.

He was always happy and friendly, and was known in his youth as a strong guinea pig who could carry cucumbers.

His hobby was eating almonds and sitting and thinking.

Mr.Muffin is survived by his six children, all of whom have left home and married, and countless numbers of grandchildren who live here, there and everywhere.

Mr. Muffin will be sorely missed.

United forever.

(Reuters)

Now Mr. Muffin is lying with his paws in the air, his nose stiff and cold.

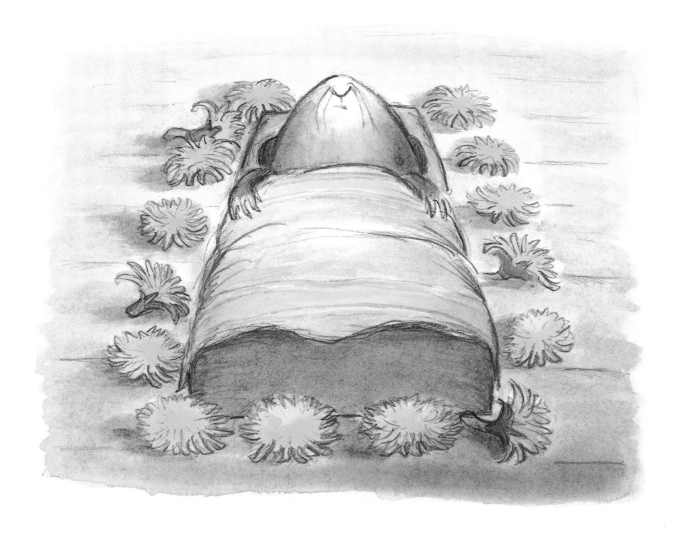

He is covered with a handkerchief, and fifteen dandelion blossoms are placed round him. Dandelions were his favourite flowers.

Then he is carefully laid in a cardboard box lined with beautiful, soft moss. And beside him are the things he loved most:

A small clay guinea pig that looks just like Victoria, a picture of six, sweet little children, a few almonds and crackers, and a piece of cucumber. And the last letter of all.

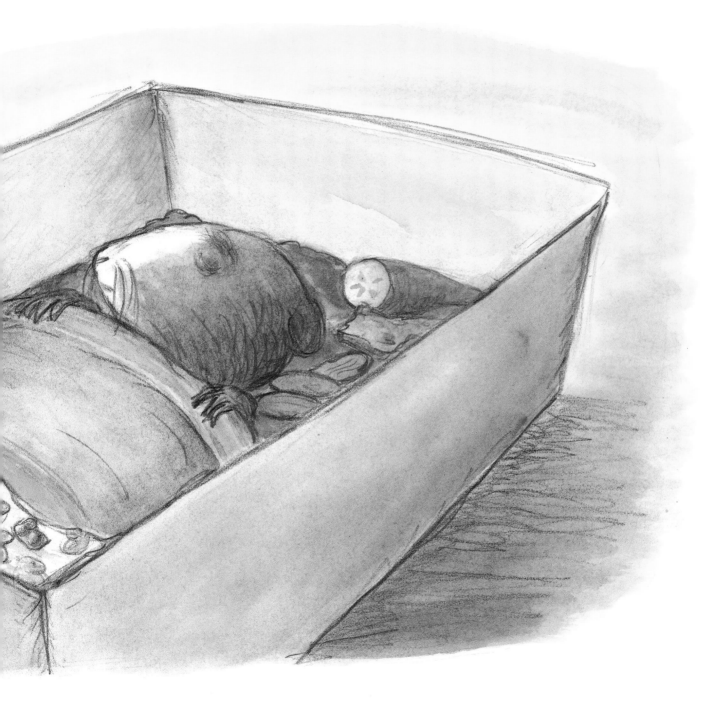

Now a hole is dug in the ground in a corner of the garden. A bird sings a mournful song.

It is cloudy and dark, and a cold wind blows through the world.

Many mourners weep at Mr. Muffin's grave. The whole country is in mourning. Maybe the king will come, and the queen too. Maybe the funeral will be broadcast live on television and radio. Maybe. A fine cross and many flowers. Wreaths of dandelions for Mr. Muffin with the words: 'Thanks for everything.'

A daddy is saying 'It was with shock and sadness that we learned of Mr. Muffin's passing.' There's a tear in his eye. Everybody cries. A girl plays *The Lord is my Shepherd* on the recorder. Some children sing the only song they can think of right now: 'Happy birthday to you, happy birthday to you ...'

And then they sing the burial hymn.

And the sun sets and darkness falls on our peaceful garden.

Now you know more than we do, Mr. Muffin.

Now you know what happens when you die.

It's either a kind of rest, isn't it,

and if so then dying is nothing to be scared of.

Or you get taken somewhere else,

to eternal life, and you are happy there.

And then dying is something to look forward to!

Why be scared of dying?

Isn't that right, Mr. Muffin?

You know now, don't you?